Garama, Garden of the Sahara

Written by Marianne Posadas
Illustrated by Rebecca Kereopa

Contents

For learning solutions, visit cengage.com.au

Meet the Characters

Mennad

A wise engineer.

Emir Izdârasen

The ruler of Garama.

Tafalkayt

Mennad's daughter.

Ittû

Mennad's wife and Tafalkayt's mother.

Dear Reader

Before I started to write this book, I had no idea that thriving and prosperous civilisations once existed in the Sahara desert. The story of the Garamantes, who built an artificial oasis in one of the world's harshest environments, only to see it all disappear, seemed like a wonderful tale to tell, with a meaningful lesson for today's world. I hope you enjoy it!

Marianne Posadas
Author

Garama

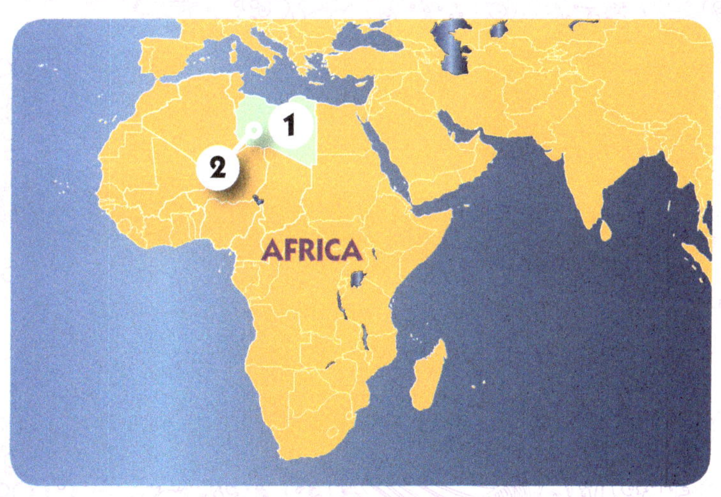

1. Modern-day Libya
2. Garama

1 Prologue

On the old woman's command, the camel carrying her knelt down. She dismounted and looked at the dry, dusty ruins that lay before her. Year after year, the relentless desert winds had blown the sands into every crevice, every corner. This place, once so lush and green, was desolate and barren. It was little more than a bleak hill in an endless sea of sand.

"Mother!" called a voice. The old woman turned. "Why are we stopping? I have studied the works of great scholars who have written of this place, and there are nothing but wild beasts here, beasts that roam the dunes and rocks. We should keep moving!"

The old woman smiled at her impatient son. For a second, she considered answering his question with another. Her father, if he'd been there, would have liked that, she thought.

"I have come to answer my father's question," she replied simply.

The young man looked around. "Here?" he said. "In the middle of nowhere?"

"To you, this may seem like the middle of nowhere," replied the old woman. "To me," she added mysteriously, "it is the middle of what once was a circle."

"As you wish," said her son with a shrug. He knew better than to try and fathom his mother's thoughts. Through her long years she had become a wise and respected teacher, and try as he might, his debates with her always ended in defeat.

The old woman drew herself up to her full height and addressed the sands, the rocks and the sun.

"The answer is knowledge," she said. At that moment, the winds of the desert took her words and carried them over the scorching earth, far off into the never-ending sky, and scattered them to the spirits. High above, in the vastness beyond, one of those spirits nodded. His soul was finally at rest, for the old woman had shown him that all things were as he had hoped they would be. She had indeed returned, and he had listened. The answer the winds carried to him was worth waiting for.

2 The Emir's Desire

In a land far away and a time long forgotten, among the shifting sands and rocky outcrops of Aṣ-Ṣahrā′ al-Kubrā, there once flourished an oasis known as Garama. There, grapes and figs grew sweet and plentiful.

Fanned by a hot westerly breeze and nourished by ancient waters brought to the surface through the shafts and tunnels of the *foggara*, fields of millet and wheat ripened, offering bread to all who lived in the villages nearby.

For six generations, Emir Izdârasen's dynasty had ruled over this island of plenty, set like a jewel in the great desert that stretched endlessly to the north, south, east and west. All that the emir and his people needed came in abundance, either from the sun, the soil or the shafts of the *foggara*.

Yet, despite the balance that had endured for hundreds of years, contentment eluded the emir. While his subjects were happy with bread, water, grapes and figs, Emir Izdârasen desired what he did not have.

During Izdârasen's reign, a boy named Mennad had been born into a family of farmers. While he learnt the ways of his forefathers, who had toiled among their crops, he showed great promise and had an aptitude for learning. He was sent far across the desert to the ancient Arabic city of al-Qayrawan, where he spent many years studying the secrets and skills of the great engineers. Upon his return to Garama, he became the emir's vizier in charge of all engineering and building works. His wisdom in overseeing the shafts and tunnels that brought water to the oasis brought him many rewards, but the two for which he was most grateful were a beautiful wife, Ittû, and a young daughter, Tafalkayt.

One day, Emir Izdârasen summoned his vizier, and Mennad appeared before him dutifully.

"Mennad, I am troubled and I seek your help," said the emir. "You have travelled to the great city of al-Qayrawan, where noble people, sultans, great soldiers and renowned teachers gather. How do they speak of our small oasis?"

"Excellency, they all know Garama as a place of abundant water, fruit, grain and sunshine," replied Mennad truthfully. He was about to say how

fortunate the Garamantes were that, amongst all the people of the north, their small oasis was well thought of, but the emir raised his hand before Mennad could continue.

"Exactly," said the emir. "Where we should have fine perfumes and precious oils, we have only water. Where we should have sapphires and diamonds, we have only fruits and grains. Where we should have silver and gold, we have only sunshine."

Mennad knew that the very existence of the oasis depended upon these simple things, but he dared not contradict Izdârasen.

The emir continued, "The traders from the south bring us salt and oil in return for what little millet and wheat we do not need. They continue

on, their saddlebags full of gold and jewels unopened, destined for the emirs of the north. We must grow so much millet and wheat that these traders will pay us in gold and jewels, not mere salt and oil."

Mennad knew that the people of Garama had no use for gold and jewels, and that unlike salt and oil, they would not make their daily bread taste better. But again, he dared not contradict his ruler.

"Excellency, I was once a farmer, and I know that there is little room between stalks of grain growing in a field. How should we grow more millet and wheat in fields that are already full?"

"We need more fields," replied the emir.

"But that will mean more water," said Mennad.

Izdârasen nodded. "And so we arrive at the reason you have been summoned here today."

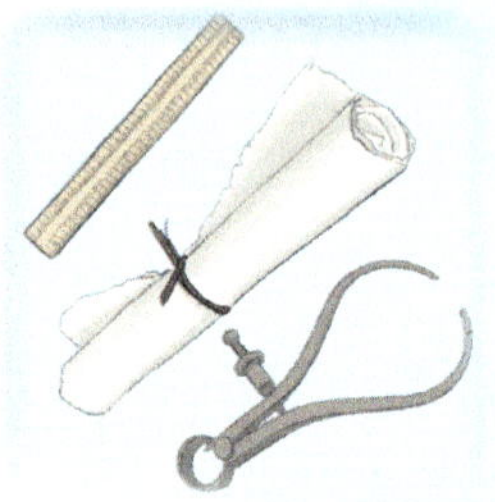

3 The Most Precious Thing

Tafalkayt could see that her father was troubled upon his return from the emir's palace, and knowing that a worry shared is a worry halved, she followed him to the courtyard and asked him what weighed so heavily on his mind.

"Dear child," replied Mennad. "Let me ask you a question instead. In all of Garama, what is the most precious thing we have?"

Tafalkayt thought carefully. "Surely it is the bread that sustains us every day," she replied.

Mennad shook his head. "There is something more precious that comes before the bread," he said.

"Wheat!" said Tafalkayt. "Wheat is our most precious thing."

Again, Mennad shook his head. "It comes even before wheat," he said.

"Sunshine to ripen the harvest," ventured Tafalkayt.

"There is sunshine throughout the great desert," replied Mennad. "Yet there is nothing precious there. Think again."

Tafalkayt smiled. "It is water, father. I should have guessed. You think of little else but water, with your tunnels and shafts burrowing deep into the rock."

"You are right, child, in both respects. Water is our most precious thing, and all who live within our oasis should be pleased that I think of little else, for it is those thoughts on which they depend."

Tafalkayt nodded in agreement.

"Unfortunately, Emir Izdârasen wishes to swap our most precious thing for shiny baubles of silver and gold. I must triple our water supply to grow three times as many fields of millet and wheat," explained Mennad.

"But there will still be plenty of water and bread for those who live within Garama," shrugged Tafalkayt. "So why do you struggle with the emir's vision?"

Mennad laughed. "You sound just like Izdârasen himself," he said. His face grew serious. "The problem, my child, is that tripling the water supply means the reservoir will last barely one-third of its current life."

"But the water has been coming out of the *foggara* for years," protested Tafalkayt. "It will surely last forever!"

Mennad shook his head. "I fear not, my dear child. One day soon, the *foggara* may run dry. Look around you." He stood, and swept his hand across the endless expanse of the great desert beyond the walls of the courtyard. "For all those years, when has there ever been any rain to replenish the reservoir?"

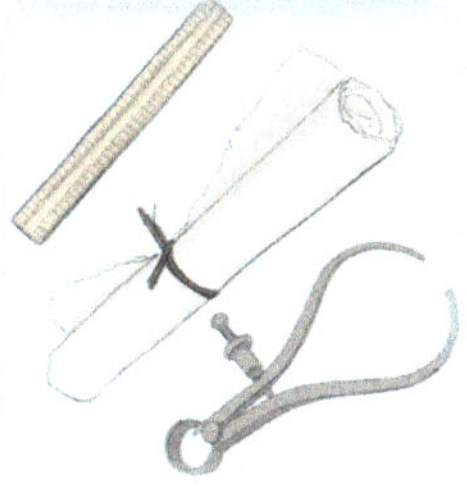

Despite his concerns, Mennad did as the emir ordered, and one month hence he found himself back in Izdârasen's palace. He brought with him plans, calculations and lists, and he laid these before the emir.

"As your chief engineer, Emir Izdârasen, I must tell you that all of these plans are possible. But it will take many seasons for our slaves and prisoners to dig the shafts and tunnels to enlarge the *foggara*'s network. I fear that the first crops from the new fields will not arrive before ten years."

Izdârasen was not interested in Mennad's plans and calculations. His desire for precious things grew more urgent with each passing day, like a fire that had grown out of control, consuming first grasses, then twigs and sticks, then entire trees in its hunger.

"Then we must have more slaves and prisoners," he said. "If our present number will take ten years,

does it not follow that ten times that number will only take one year?"

Mennad's discomfort grew. "That is true, Excellency, but this extra labour will require extra food and water."

"And as they dig and we see the fruits of their efforts, so shall we increase our supply of both," replied the emir.

"Excellency," began Mennad, but he was silenced with a wave of the emir's hand.

"Vizier, you have given me your plans, calculations and lists, for these are the things with which an engineer must properly concern himself," said Izdârasen. "And I," he continued, "shall give you the prisoners and slaves to carry out these works,

for these are the things with which an emir must properly concern himself."

"As you wish," bowed Mennad.

And so it was that, within days, the emir gathered his finest soldiers and his ablest charioteers and dispatched them to the lands of those who lived far beyond the great desert of Aṣ-Ṣahrā′ al-Kubrā with orders to return with a multitude of prisoners and slaves. In all directions, great clouds of dust and sand could be seen rising, as horses, chariots and soldiers spread north, south, east and west through the desert.

From his palace, the emir watched with great anticipation in his heart but, blinded by his hunger for gold and silver and jewels, the troubled cloud that swirled around the heart of his vizier was invisible to him.

4 A Foolish Spiral

As the weeks turned into months, Mennad grew distant from his wife, Ittû, and his daughter Tafalkayt, surrounding himself with bigger plans and greater calculations and longer lists. Despite his forebodings, he knew he could not fail in the task the emir had set him.

During the day, beneath the scorching sun, Mennad oversaw the labours of the prisoners and slaves that the emir had supplied him in abundance. At the outer edges of the *foggara*, he ordered that deep vertical shafts should be dug into the rock every ten paces and that once water was reached, tunnels should be

burrowed, both back to the existing *foggara* and in the direction of the next shaft.

The giant network of tunnels crept outwards from Garama, and drop by precious drop, the flow of the underground water they channelled back to the oasis continued. But Mennad could see that it was growing harder to reach what little water they found. Where once it had taken ten metres for a shaft to reach water, now it took thirty. And, instead of greatly increasing the flow of water, the supply was, in fact, imperceptibly growing smaller and smaller.

At night, exhausted, thirsty and hungry, throngs of prisoners and slaves retired to the large camps that had been set up on the edge of the desert.

One evening, upon his return from one of the camps, Mennad too was weary and hungry. He had not eaten since sunrise, so Ittû and Tafalkayt prepared a simple supper of grapes and olives. Since the hundreds of slaves and prisoners had arrived, food had become scarce, but Emir Izdârasen had dismissed the concerns of his people, saying that once new water flowed onto newly sown fields, the times of plenty would return once more.

Ittû and Tafalkayt, who had watched Mennad grow more and more troubled, were not convinced by the emir's promises.

"When will Garama once again have bread, water, grapes and figs aplenty?" asked Ittû.

"How much longer?" asked Tafalkayt.

Mennad smiled at his wife and daughter. As he had before, he did not answer their question, but posed one himself. "During my studies in al-Qayrawan, there was one thing we learned that was simple yet profound. Do you know what this thing was?"

Ittû and Tafalkayt did not know.

"To draw a perfect circle," said Mennad. "All you need is a central point, a pencil and a fixed length of string to join the two."

From the look on their faces, Mennad could see that Ittû and Tafalkayt did not understand, so he continued.

"Emir Izdârasen believes the path we are taking to fulfil his desires is a circle. More workers mean more tunnels. More tunnels mean more water. More water means more crops.

More crops mean more bread. And, at the close of his circle, more bread means he can go round once again, starting with more workers. And so it goes and goes, just like the pencil on the string."

"But do these things not follow each other, father?" asked Tafalkayt. "Surely the emir is right."

Once again, Mennad smiled. "Only if there is a fixed length of string. And in this case, the length of string is water. As the water is used up, the string becomes shorter and shorter. You will still move your pencil around, satisfied that you are drawing a fine curve. But you are no longer drawing a circle. The emir is making precisely that mistake. He thinks he is drawing a perfect circle, but alas, he is not. He is, as his string shortens, drawing a spiral. And all of us here in Garama are being pulled in along with it."

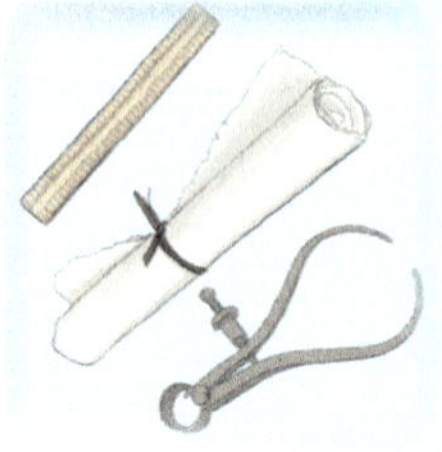

Where previously there had been enough extra millet and wheat to trade with the caravans trekking northwards, now there was none. The inhabitants of Garama had to forego the salt and oil that had once been bartered from the traders who passed through the oasis. Their bread became dry and tasteless. All of the grain was needed to feed those who toiled on the *foggara*. And although they worked from sunrise to sunset each day, their efforts were not met with equal rewards. With every ten paces the network of shafts extended further into the desert, the depth of the shafts had to be increased, as did the time it took to dig them.

Emir Izdârasen was at first alarmed to see that the flow of water into the oasis was not tripling, but in fact diminishing. But his alarm swiftly turned to displeasure. His plan had been simple, and if the plan was not flawed – and how could it be? – then its execution must be at fault.

He summoned Mennad to the palace once more. "Vizier, at the start of this endeavour, you gave me your plans, calculations and lists, for those were the things, as chief engineer, you undertook to supply," said Izdârasen. "And I," he continued, " gave you the prisoners and slaves to carry out these works, for these were the things, as emir, I undertook to supply."

Mennad knew better than to interrupt the emir. He nodded and waited for a chance to outline his concerns.

"I did not fail in my undertaking," continued the emir sternly. "From all corners of Aṣ-Ṣahrā′ al-Kubrā, my charioteers and soldiers returned with slaves and prisoners who were set to work the length of each day. And so they have done, for each one of the past twelve months." Izdârasen paused, and appeared to be thinking. Then he switched his gaze back to Mennad. He frowned. "Yet still there is not the water I demanded. Therefore, as one of us completed their obligations, the other must necessarily have failed."

"Excellency," started Mennad, but the emir had convinced himself that the logic of his argument was infallible.

"I recall your words, twelve months since, when we first talked of this," said the emir. "You declared that Garama was known as a place of abundant water, fruit, grain and sunshine. And I replied that where we should have fine perfumes and precious oils, we had only water. Where we should have sapphires and diamonds, we had only fruits and grains. Where we should have silver and gold, we had only sunshine."

"You did, Excellency," said Mennad.

A chilling tone came into the emir's voice, and he started to tremble with fury. "Then why is it that, despite the efforts of hundreds of workers, we now have none of those things bar one?"

"Excellency, I ..." started Mennad.

"Should I leave you to complete your works, will I discover that in another twelve months you have also managed to extinguish the sunshine?" roared the emir.

Mennad summoned up all his courage. He looked directly at Izdârasen. "Excellency," he said. "The sunshine is beyond the control of any engineer. At the end of the day, when the sun disappears, I cannot summon up any more sunlight because, much as we may wish for it, there is no more to be had. And so it is with water. At the end of this doomed undertaking when the water disappears, I will not be able summon any more because, much as our parched crops and throats crave it, there will be no more to be had."

Izdârasen flew into a rage. "Each day for six generations, every person in Garama has awoken to plentiful sunlight and plentiful water," he shouted. "It has always been that way, and so it will remain for another six generations." He turned to walk to his private chambers. He looked back at Mennad. "Vizier, you have three months. If you fail, your family will be the first to suffer. Do not disappoint me."

5 A Final Question

Mennad gazed out at the shifting sands and rocky outcrops of Aṣ-Ṣahrā′ al-Kubrā.

Far from Garama, a group of workers struggled to haul buckets of rock and sand from the shaft. The long dark hole was over fifty metres deep. It was back-breaking work, yet still there was no sign of water.

Over the dunes, Mennad saw a distant movement. As he watched, the specks on the horizon became a caravan of ten camels, led by a band of traders. Mennad had grown thin from hunger and weary from worry, but at the sight of the caravan, his heart grew lighter. This was what he had been

waiting for. Knowing that Garama no longer offered a place to rest, eat, drink and trade, the caravan traders rarely passed through on their trek north. Mennad had waited three months for one to appear. During that time, the threats of the emir had been ringing in his ears.

He struggled to his feet. Alone in the great desert, he headed eastwards towards the distant caravan. Soon, his group of workers became a speck on the horizon. The caravan drew closer and closer. Finally he hailed the traders with a hoarse shout.

That night, after the sun disappeared, Mennad returned to his house. Tafalkayt could see that her father was more troubled than usual. She asked him what weighed so heavily on his mind.

"Dear child," replied Mennad. "As I have done on so many evenings before, let me ask you a question instead. In all of Garama, what is the most precious thing we have?"

Tafalkayt smiled. "Father, you have asked me that question before and I remember your answer well. Water is our most precious thing, and all who live within our oasis depend upon it."

Mennad looked at his daughter and there was great sadness in his eyes.

"And when I gave you that answer, I truly believed it," he said. "But I was wrong."

Tafalkayt stared at her father. What could he mean?

"The most precious thing we have is our family," said Mennad. "You, my daughter, and my wife, Ittû. I might travel to the edges of Aṣ-Ṣahrā′ al-Kubrā and beyond, and yet I would find nothing more precious."

Tafalkayt looked at her father and saw a tear rolling down his dry, gaunt cheek. "Fetch your mother, child," he said, wiping his face and standing up. "And then fill your pockets with whatever small things you may wish to remember this place by."

“What do you mean, father?” asked Tafalkayt. “Where are we going?”

“I am going nowhere,” replied Mennad. “If I leave, the emir will send soldiers to chase me to the ends of the Earth.” He smiled at his daughter. “But my most precious loved ones are going to a place where they may once more find the simple happiness that comes with bread, water, grapes and figs. Hurry now. The caravan is waiting.”

“But when will we return?” asked Tafalkayt. “Where is this caravan going? Why are we leaving?”

“You know I only ever answer a question with a question, my child,” smiled Mennad. “And so here is your question.”

Tafalkayt waited, while her father chose his words carefully. “The circle of the emir’s dream will vanish because the string that describes it is spun of ignorance,” he said finally. “As you draw your circle of life, what string should you use to make sure your pencil moves ever outwards, not inwards?”

Tafalkayt stared at her father, bewildered. “I shall await your answer, my child,” said Mennad, turning his back so she would see no more tears. “Take your time and do not worry. This is where you began your circle, and I know that you will pass by this place once more. And when you do, I shall be listening.”

Author's Note

Garama was the ancient centre of a civilisation in what is now southern Libya. Surrounded by the Sahara Desert, or As-Sahra´ al-Kubra, as it is known in Arabic, the civilisation flourished for five hundred years by tapping huge reservoirs of groundwater. Thousands of kilometres of subterranean tunnels, known as *foggara*, were built by slaves and prisoners over the centuries, and it is estimated that over 140 billion litres of water were extracted from rock beneath the Sahara Desert. Unfortunately, groundwater is a non-renewable resource, and once the supply was exhausted, the Garamante civilisation withered and disappeared. The Garamantes were included in the first western historical work, which was written by the ancient Greek historian, Herodotus:

"To the southward, in the part of Libya where wild beasts are found, live the Garamantes, who avoid all interaction with others.

At ten days' distance, there is a hill of salt with water, as well as a great number of palms which are exceedingly productive. This place is inhabited by numerous people, who cover the beds of salt with earth, and then plant it. Among them live a species of oxen, which walk backwards while they are feeding; their horns are so formed that they cannot do otherwise. They are so long and curved in such a manner that if they did not recede as they fed, they would stick in the ground. Garamantes, sitting in carriages drawn by four horses, give chase to desert cave dwellers, who, of all the people in the world of whom we have ever heard, are far the swiftest of foot: their food is lizard, serpent and other reptile; their language bears no resemblance to that of any other, for it is like the screaming of bats."

Adapted from *The Histories*,

Herodotus (c. 484 BC – c. 425 BC)

The answer
the winds carried to him
was worth waiting for.